FLIP-FLOP
and
Don't Stop
the story of GiGi the gymnast

written by

Darleen Anderson

illustrated by

Brittney Anderson Ferguson

Publishing Coordinator – Sharon Kizziah-Holmes

Published by Kids Book Press
An imprint of A & S Publishing, A & S Holmes, Inc.
Springfield, Missouri
Sharon Kizziah-Holmes – Publishing Coordinator

ISBN -13: 978-1-951772-89-5

DEDICATION

To daughter Gayle, whose early antics inspired the writing of this book.

You committed yourself to fourteen years of flip-flopping and was an integral part of helping the dynamic, exciting and beautiful sport of gymnastic become what it is today.

GiGi the gymnast...

makes her mother gasp.

Everyday it's, thump - flop.

"Stop! Stop!"

So GiGi does somersaults on the bed.

When sent to the corner, she
stands on her head

She uses her hands for walking...

more than she does her feet.

She sits in the splits,

instead of a seat.

Her mother says, "GiGi, you really must stop!

You'll wreck the house, the way you flop."

Thump - flop.

"Stop! Stop!"

GiGi went outside to do cartwheels and rolls.

Until she knocked down her dad's tomato poles.

The garden was no place to do jumps and leaps.

She ended up squashing the green beans and beets.

Thump - flop.

"Stop! Stop!"

"Please do your flopping on the front lawn."

And that she did, from the brink of dawn.

She vaulted onto a hedge...

and did scary handstands on the ledge.

Thump - flop.

"Stop! Stop!"

Mother and Dad had a long talk.

GiGi would never be happy just to sit or walk.

They must find a place where GiGi can train...

to improve her body as well as her brain.

Sure enough, there it was, GiGi's own dream.

A gym with uneven parallel bars,
a vaulting horse, trampoline and beam.

There was a coach to teach GiGi just how to move...

in a beautiful way, so graceful and smooth.

GiGi is a real gymnast now. She really can go!

See how straight she keeps her knees and points
each and every toe?

She can do mounts and dismounts, too.

Wraps, kips and other tricks new.

She has grown in strength and is also tough.

She knows about rippers, chalking up and stuff.

At exam time she was in great
condition and well-exercised.

GiGi's doctor was happily surprised!

Now everyone is happy, and here's what she hears.

"Go ahead flip - flopping and don't stop, dear."

Flip - flop, and don't stop!

About the Author

For Darleen Anderson, retirement from a career of teaching beginning readers, did not mean she would stop helping children become life-long readers. She continues her mission of searching for the right book, for the right child at the right time.   She continues to write short stories and poetry and is a volunteer reader for schools and nurseries.

Darleen resides in the beautiful Ozarks with her husband Bill. Her two grown children, five grandchildren and fifteen great grands live nearby. Life is good.

ABOUT THE ILLUSTRATOR

Brittney Anderson Ferguson has been illustrating for her author grandmother, Darleen, since she was in grade school. She didn't hesitate to say yes, when asked to illustrate this book. She continues to use her art talent in sewing, interior decorating and painting.

She was a high-level, competitive gymnast before becoming a certified cosmetologist, the mother of three sons and twin daughters. Brittney also calls the Ozarks home.

Made in the USA
Columbia, SC
27 April 2022